BEDTIME HORRORS

For Adults & Young Adults
Volume One

NIC KRISTOFER BLACK

WITH ILLUSTRATIONS BY JORGE GONZALEZ

Author
NIC KRISTOFER BLACK

Illustrations and Cover Art
JORGE GONZALEZ

Design and Layout
NIC KRISTOFER BLACK

Line Editor
ANNA STORM

Production
CHRISTOPHER J. CACCIACARNE

ZOMBIE HOLOCAUST courtesy of Sinsterfonts.com
Steelfish courtesy of Typodermicfonts.com
PIRULEN courtesy of Typodermicfonts.com

PREMIERE EDITION

EACH TALE IN THIS COLLECTION IS ONE PAGE
LONG AND EXACTLY 1000 WORDS IN LENGTH,
BASED ON MICROSOFT WORD COUNT
METHODOLOGY.

For more information about this book, future
publications as well as promotions, please visit:
www.bedtime-horrors.com

The phrase **"Bedtime Horrors"** is a trademark of
INTERNEGATIVE LLC.

WWW.BEDTIME-HORRORS.COM

CONTENTS

6 A Claw At The Closet Door

10 Creature, I

14 Greyhound Bus

18 Job Order

22 Monster In The Brush

26 Creature, II

30 Spare Parts

34 The Life Raft

38 Glass Jars

42 Creature, III

With a slight tremor, MacRae's hand finds the martini, raising it
to his lips for one final sip. Moments later, a creature from
the blackest recesses of nightmares smashes
through the window.

A CLAW AT THE CLOSET DOOR

SPIDER-MAN NIGHTLIGHT dimly illuminates the room, as glow-in-the-dark stars strewn across the wall and ceiling cast a blissful gaze onto the slumbering boy. However, under the turquoise blankets little Kiki is actually quite awake and light-years away from any feelings of bliss.

Most of the blankets are already pulled up tightly around his neck, and he tucks the rest under his arms and legs, forming a cocoon between himself and the outside world. Motionless, he tries not to breath, move, not even swallow for fear of waking the monster in his closet.

Three years ago and counting, Mom explained and reasoned and exhausted herself in various attempts to convince Kiki that there was no such thing as monsters. Yet dutifully, every night, the boy would drag his toy box in front of the closet "just in case."

Then came his eighth birthday.

Right at Kiki's feet, Mom placed an unexpected present, clad in dark foreboding giftwrap and a lurid bow of betrayal: "There is no such thing as monsters and the toy box will not be dragged in front of the closet again." Staring at the grotesque 'gift' laid out before him, Kiki's large brown eyes grew even larger. But there was more. "This will hurt me more than it hurts you, but move the toy box again, and so help me, you'll be spending an entire night inside your closet full of imaginary monsters!" Taking one terrified step backwards and away from his mother, he was absolutely baffled by what, in his child's mind, seemed to be capricious malevolence. "Mommy please," Kiki pleaded, insisting, "there is a monster." But this time Mom wouldn't budge. "Tough love," she thought.

So Kiki had spent the last four evenings under the blankets, trembling with apprehension, determined not to let his eyes close even for a second. For an eight-year-old, he'd made a valiant effort. But as midnight arrives on night five, his eyelids have become a pair of roller shades, little by little sliding shut. Mere seconds later, what he has been desperate to avoid, happens: The smallest of snores, a half-snore, quietly slips from his nostrils.

Almost immediately, his eyes spring open.

Filled with distress, he scans the room, waiting until the very last to allow his gaze to fall upon the dreaded closet door. How long had he been dozing? How long had he let his guard down? As it turns out just long enough. Nearly imperceptibly, the slow, twisting, mechanical clacks of the closet doorknob fill the tiny room. Moments later a long creeaaaak emanates from the door hinges, sending chills through Kiki's small, bone-weary body. Brow plowed with furrows of anxiety, he swiftly squeezes his eyelids shut. If he keeps them closed tightly enough, he reasons, once he reopens them, whatever is there may be gone. Just maybe.

After a far too short moment of suspended terror, one eyelid squints open. A long black crack — maybe 3 inches wide — presents itself where the closet door has been slid ajar. At that moment, Kiki's heart races. But it is nothing like the pounding that follows as he sees three daggered, hairy, claws slyly curl out of the crack. Kiki pulls the blankets up to his eyes, flattening his body in an attempt to make the bed appear unoccupied. Slowly, cautiously, the creature swings both closet doors fully open. In the glow of the nightlight, the creature's proboscis sniffs the air: It can smell 'little boy' and this causes saliva to ooze from the corners o its mandibles. Fleetly, the creature plods out of the shadows of the closet.

As if the toy box were the tiny coffin that would soor hold the boy's remains, the creature cleverly mimics wha Kiki has done so many nights before, but instead, drags the box directly in front of the bedroom door. Desperatel hungry, the creature wants absolutely nothing interfering with its midnight snack. As its face morphs into an expression that can only be described as famished glee, the creature turns, lumbering toward the bed!

Kiki hysterically scoots backwards, kicking away his blankets. Springs on the little twin mattress bow as the creature pounds the far end of the bed, tilting everything a the top towards its mouth. "You look tasty." The creature snarls in a deep whisper (fully cognizant of Kiki's parents ir the adjacent room). Kiki struggles to hold onto the headboard as his pillow and a stuffed animal tumble into the creature's maw. "You look TASTY!"

The creature's growl is interrupted by a long, gooe tongue springing from the gaping hole that is its mouth Lukewarm and slimy, the tongue wraps around the boy's bare ankle, yanking with ferocity. Kiki's left hand slips from one side of the headboard and only three fingers of his righ hand desperately clench the other. Each blast of the creature's fetid breath coats his body with slimy condensation As he feels his grip about to give way, Kiki screams louc and long. Unexpectedly, a roar coming from beneath the bed joins his desperate cry for help.

Forcing back tears, Kiki glances over his shoulder. Fou thick appendages sprout from underneath the bed, locking around the creature's arms and torso. A fifth appendage shoots out, wrapping the creature's throat tightly. Abruptly the wretched tongue releases Kiki's foot and the tilted bec crashes back to the floor. Violently thrashing, the creature is dragged underneath. Atop the bed and crouched on al fours, Kiki is heaved and jostled about. Then, with severa percussive crunches and a mammoth groan, the room falls still.

Kiki peeks furtively over the edge of the mattress just ir time to see a suctioned appendage curl back into the darkness. A muffled gurgling follows as caustic acids sluice through the tentacled creature's digestive system. Finally all is silent, that is, besides the calm breathing of a relievec eight-year-old. Luckily for the boy, although there had beer a monster in his closet, there was a much bigger one living under his bed.

A CLAW AT THE CLOSET DOOR 9

CREATURE. I

REAKING AND GROANING under massive pressure, the submersible touches down parallel to the wounded *HMS Vengeance.* Lindbrook uses the sleeve of his wetsuit to swirl away a clear patch on the fog-laden porthole. "That thing's massive," he mumbles. And he's right.

Lying on its side, the 150-meter Vanguard-class submarine is manned by 135 crewmen and carries amongst its armament a lethal payload of Trident D5 ballistic missiles. When communications dropped off 22 hours ago there was restrained cause for alarm. Three hours later, when the vessel's emergency beacon blipped on, the Royal Navy hastily dispatched S Squadron.

Lindbrook is a civilian contractor and the only member of the team to have piloted a DSRV to this depth. After 27 similar dives, he could practically do this in the deepest of sleeps.

Maneuvering languidly through hypothermic waters, the squadron surveys the fatally wounded sub. "Looks like whatever happened, they scraped that formation over there. Compromised the pressure hull. End of story." The Commander's tone is steady, unemotional. "Consider yourselves warned: There's a 99.999% chance we're gonna see a lot of 'floaters.' And I will give you my personal guarantee it's gonna be freakier than anything you've ever seen. So in advance, I'm giving you permission to piss your pants. Fortunately, we're already under water."

With the vessel on its side, two cutting torches begin the work of producing an opening sizable enough for the men to gain access. As they slide clear the serrated metal sheet, the squadron's torches probe the darkness of the sub's interior, revealing what the Commander had warned of — a floating cemetery. As far back as their beams reach, decaying bodies slowly twist in the murky waters. Barely keeping trepidation at bay, the team moves forward. At the rear, maneuvering through the wreckage, Lindbrook is unnerved to see not only has the sub's crew drowned, but some are missing limbs, others, chunks of their faces.

"Keep up, Lindbrook," the Commander barks. "We're not here to sightsee. Thought you were checked out for gigs like this?"

"Yeah, copy that. Never seen bodies in this bad a shape though. I mean it's been less than 36 hours." Pulling one of the corpses near, Lindbrook pokes a finger into a hole in its forehead. "And check this out. Looks like this one 'drowned' from a bullet to the head. Make any sense to you?"

"You're our driver," the Commander intones in an effort to still the team's increasingly jittery nerves. He breaks loose the wheel on the port door leading to the next compartment. "If being here is wiggin' you out then, be my guest, wait for us back in the submerse—ackkk!"

Swiftly shifting their attention from Lindbrook, the men see the Commander painfully gripping his arm. One of the floating corpses has emerged from the port door and sunk its rotting teeth into the Commander's dive suit. Blood begins saturating the water. "What the…?" mutters Lindbrook. Less than a moment passes before more decaying bodies begin pouring from the airlock. "Zombies! I knew it! Everybody move!" Understandably, panicked expletives begin to fill the transmissions in the team's dive helmets. While Lindbrook swiftly puts himself on a course to exit the ship, a backwards glance reveals the squadron bogged down, waging a fruitless, slow-motion skirmish in an attempt to save the Commander — and having failed that, themselves.

Lungs burning, Lindbrook reaches the opening leading outside the sub. More than partway through the portal a pale, decaying hand grasps his leg, pulling him back inside. Wide-eyed, he pulls his dive knife, cleanly lopping off the zombie's arm. Hurriedly, he exits. Only a few strokes behind, a dozen zombies squirm to exit the hull. Terror presses beads of cold sweat from the pores of Lindbrook's forehead.

Attracted by the chum-laden waters, a full-grown tiger shark emerges from the darkness, disrupting the eerie fray. Its jaws quickly devour several of the creatures. Having been given a slight reprieve, Lindbrook closes in on the submersible's roof hatch. But like a disturbed anthill, zombies continue pouring from the submarine's hull, latching onto the shark and finally dragging it to the darkness of the seafloor.

As the sub's wound continues disgorging putrefied creatures, two branches of zombies stretch into the gloom of the sea: One branch extends towards the seafloor and the other towards Lindbrook. With the sounds of his own labored panting filling his dive helmet, his right flipper is suddenly tugged from his foot. Glancing back, he meets yellow eyes lifelessly staring into his. Lindbrook lands two frenzied kicks. As he reaches the submersibles airlock, fatigued muscles spin the hatch wheel much slower than he'd like them to. A string of zombies is mere heartbeats away.

Maneuvering himself inside, Lindbrook pulls at the airlock. To his dread, another force strains in the opposite direction. One of the creatures has thrust its head inside of the craft. "No! No!" Lindbrook howls. Then, like some gruesome avenger, the rotting head of the tiger shark appears in the port window. Now 'zombified,' its jagged teeth have already ravaged one of the creatures and within moments chomp the second in half.

Legs severed, the zombie's torso spills into the compartment. Lindbrook pounds a large red plunger, sealing the airlock. From behind, however, the creature's arms quickly entangle his. As water drains from the compartment, Lindbrook stumbles backwards, unrelentingly slamming the zombie against the submersible's metal walls. Terrifying moments later, the severely injured torso tumbles to the ground — facedown, guts exposed. He uses a fire axe and the last surges of adrenalin to finish what the shark started.

SPRAWLED BREATHLESSLY on the floor, Linbrook's fingers find the Emergency Unmanned Resurface actuator. Tilting slightly forward, the craft begins a slow ascent. Pulling his weary arm back from the controls, Lindbrook's eyes fatefully glimpse teeth marks gashed into the side of his palm. Outside, in the bleakness of the deep, all is silent except for the sound of tortured laughter echoing from inside the steel walls of the submersible.

12 CREATURE, I

GREYHOUND BUS

F ROM THE WATER TOWER it's easy to see that, upon impact, the flying saucer sliced deeply into the frozen ground — like a knife into piecrust. Unfortunately, following the close of the rendering plant, those who remained in town lacked sufficient curiosity to poke their noses into anything that didn't directly affect the gutted remains of their previous lives. Thus, the crash had gone unnoticed.

The alien ship, jutting only a few meters above the ground, is really not much of a flying saucer. Fitted with condenser fins several times larger than the ship's engines, its appearance can only be described as a slightly flattened, refrigerated orb. That's because Aminodynes possess heavy liquid bodies — essentially an ICEE slush drink wrapped inside of a membrane.

Leaving behind a trail of blue, quickly thawing fluid, the surviving creature has begun sloshing its way across the compacted dirt. With its membrane ruptured, if it does not quickly find a place to contain its bodily structure, it will meet a fate similar to its fellow crewmembers.

But for Greyhound bus driver William Henderson, the Aminodyne is the least of his worries.

After a long haul he parks in the station's rear lot, eager to return to a very ill wife. One hand finds the white paper sack he placed inside a cup holder. As his knees brace to stand, his neck is suddenly obliged to turn in the direction of "tek," "tek," "tek" on the door glass. His eyes first meet the barrel of a shotgun and next the mouth-breathing glower of two mountain men. Slowly cranking the door open, the men jangle up the stairs of the bus.

"You ain't done for the night right yet," drawls the taller man. "Get back in the saddle." A choking mixture of sweat and body odor climbs aboard behind them. The shorter of the duo has a gash above his right eye. Both men's coveralls are soaked in blood. "Git us outside town limits." Then, settling the rifle barrel below the driver's ear, he finishes, "Play nice and ya just might get to keep that head of yours." So with the squeak of the airbrakes, the driver puts the bus in motion. Standing and swaying with each turn, the men speak in mutely excited tones.

"We kilt a deputy. He's deyad! Deyad!" Spurts the shorter one.

"Now hold on. I didn't kill nobody!"

"He knew'd about the meth! He woulda come up the mountain with the sheriff, FBI, ATF..."

"He stopped us for expired plates you freakin,' paranoid junkie!"

"Well whatdowedo now? He's straight kilt."

"No choice. Gonna have to move the family. Ain't safe."

"How we gonna do that?"

"I don't know, bright eyes, you tell me!"

"Okay, okay. What about the bus? Yeah, yeah this bus is like, realll big. Five times bigger than the Chevy."

"Uh huh. I gotcha. We could tie some stuff on the roof, the 'equipment' stows underneath..."

"We'd be drivin' in style like rich folk!"

"Hey, driver!" The taller one growled, "We got a stop to make."

WITH THE GREYHOUND having barely traversed the dirt road's treacherous grade, its headlights reveal a dilapidated wooden structure. After the men twice beckon, "it's safe," two women, a teenage boy and a smaller child slink into the muddy, tire-tracked front yard. All are missing teeth or have malformed features, clearly indicating a few too many shared genetic markers.

Fifty-five minutes later the over-laden bus has worked its way back down the mountain, speeding its way towards the Kentucky state line. Summoning his last reserves of courage, the driver removes his foot from the gas and begins slowly pulling the bus onto the shoulder. "Pray tell, driver, exactly what the hell are you doing?" snarls the taller one, now stomping towards the front of the bus. "This is far as I can go," the driver manages. "I've got a sick wife back home. I'm sorry. Take the bus. Do what you have to. I swear I won't report it."

RAAFFF! The butt of the rifle strikes the driver, slamming his head again the side window. "If you don't git this vehicle moving, your sick wife's gonna have a *dead* husband!" Saliva hisses through the holes left by missing teeth. "Get up here, Lloyd! Make yourself useful!" The taller one shoves the rifle into the teen boy's hands and turns toward the bus' rear lavatory. "If he does anything stupid, send him to God."

Inside the lavatory the taller one starts a much-overdue bowel movement. As he empties himself, he lets out a guttural exhalation, feeling the cold chemical mixture splash against his backside. The chill from the liquid quickly begins traveling to his thigh and then curiously to his navel. Glancing down, he's startled to see blue liquid oozing its way up his torso. Struggling to stand, he slips in the liquid pooling on the floor. As he desperately bangs for help, the fluid flows up his body, converges around his face and enters his throat.

Yanking at the door, the shorter one is flattened as the hinges snap, spilling the Aminodyne's writhing living body into the main compartment. As the Greyhound races across a wooden truss bridge, the driver's rearview mirror displays a grisly scene of blue liquid engulfing and liquefying one hapless inbred after another, screams choked under a gurgle of slushy liquid. A chill tickles his ankle, as rivulets of the liquid have made their way to the front of the bus.

Frigid winds buffet the driver's face as he swings the side door wide-open. Making the sign of the cross, he cranks the steering wheel to the left and dives to the right. The Greyhound plunges a good 250 feet before smashing through the surface of the frozen lake.

Painfully, the driver picks up his bruised, battered body. With one wobbly foot in front of the other, he begins making his way down the highway — one hand holding his jacket closed and the other clutching a white prescription bag.

GREYHOUND BUS 17

JOB ORDER

G RAXYL IS 463 YEARS OLD. Of the five distinct families of monsters, it is most difficult growing old as a Prowler. It's a fact they stubbornly deny, but is truthful nonetheless. For example, Eaves Croucher *(L. creatura attikos)* have it pretty well.

Usually small and compact, they infest tight, enclosed spaces, especially in older homes. They are the rustling under a child's bed or the clumsy bump that awakens one at night. If a home is suffering from an infestation, it's usually best to keep closet doors locked securely. Especially during the late evening hours.

Shadow Phantasms *(L. spectre pheriphereia)* commonly appear on the corner of one's eye or in the reflection of a mirror. It is that momentary glimpse that makes them particularly unsettling though they are ultimately harmless. It is suspected that these painfully shy creatures are just as terrified of seeing humans as humans are of them.

Abandons *(L. kabalos hollow)* can be found dwelling under bridges, dilapidated building structures and, very often, hollow tree stumps. Incidentally, these creatures have gained much notoriety around campfires, and have been mistakenly given names like 'troll' or 'goblin.' Teenage campers are often oblivious to the fact that being overheard calling the easily offended creatures such insulting names is often what precipitates an attack.

Vaporghouls *(L. monstrom khaos)* are winged creatures slightly larger than hummingbirds but smaller than crows. Able to vaporize their bodies at will, they float through the ether, gaining access to slumbering victims via their nostrils. Inside the mind, they masterfully twist dreams into nightmares.

When each genus of creature has lived the length of its frightful existence, either of two things happens: 1) The creature simply crumbles into nothingness and is carried away on the wind. 2) They are promptly eaten by the younger of their species.

Rare and reclusive, Prowlers *(L. creatura ultimare)* are a distinctively different stripe of creature. They exist solely to deal with the incorrigibly evil: spoiled children, corrupt businessmen, cheating spouses, felons, terrorists, murderers — that sort of ilk. There is certain, painful misfortune due to anyone who happens to see a Prowler in the corner of his or her eye. They are revered as 'monarchs of the night' and creatures from every genus often gather to watch them stalk a deserving prey.

And that reverence is what makes getting old so difficult.

Having been dropped into his stalactite-riddle cavern earlier that evening, Graxyl scans job order Z81191F but can't help noticing the bulge in his mid-section. He slips off his reading glasses, hoping that the thick lenses have somehow distorted its size. Alas, they have not. In fact, the fur running lengthwise down his back is mottled with grey. Squinting, he shifts his eyes towards the mirror fragments fixed to the cavern wall.

Rearing his head, he growls. It's scary, but not wet-one's-pants-scary as it was previously. Bringing his eyes back in line with the mirror, he winces at the worn nubs sitting sparsely atop blackened gums. His claws are a dull yellow, full of minute, dirt-filled fissures. Of course the lifespan of Prowlers is 443 years. And at 463, Graxyl is clearly on borrowed time.

But there *is* this one last job order to fill.

From atop an old stump his paws fumble with a pair of periodontal attachments. Reaching into a shallow crevice, he extricates white semi-gloss spray paint and with smooth back-and-forth motions returns his hide to a reasonably youthful tone. Methodically, he glues long, 10-inch claws over what is left of his. Standing sideways in front of the mirror, he sucks in his stomach and pushes out his chest. Clearing his throat, he inhales though his nose, slowly filling all six of his bronchial cavities. Turning to face himself squarely in the mirror, he bellows a thunderous roar. From the center of the mirror fragments, cracks branch out in all directions, rendering them nearly useless for viewing. But in the slivers left intact, a huge toothy grin reflects back at Graxyl.

He congratulates himself.

As his eyes scan the final details of job order Z81191F, he knows that tonight's prowl will probably be his last.

ASCENDING INTO THE NIGHT, reserves of strength surge through Graxyl. His hind paws track the moonlit trail, entering the mouth of the cement-lined aqueduct, leading finally up onto the neighborhood street. Stealthily, creatures of the night fall in behind Graxyl in hopes of seeing the show. Lumbering along, carefully evading the glow of the mercury vapor street lamps, he slinks alongside the parked vehicles, finally stopping at a BMW SUV displaying four silhouetted images in its rear windshield: a man, a woman, a little girl, and a cat. However, the stillness of the night is quickly broken by the abrupt clack of a house door opening.

"Rob, that was amazing," Courtney giggles, kissing the figure hanging hesitantly in the shadows of the entryway.

"Easy babe…" he warns, pulling her back inside to conceal a final kiss.

BEEP-BEEP! The locks on the SUV pop open. Humming to herself, Courtney slides into the driver's seat and mis-adjusts the rearview mirror. Her lipstick is smudged. In her peripheral vision a shadow fall across the front passenger seat. Trepidation delays her turning to investigate until it's far too late. Her stomach sinks as the window shatters.

Effortlessly peeling back metal body panels, first a head, then a thick hairy arm enter the vehicle. Her eyes widen as hordes of creatures — Crouchers, Vaporghouls, Abandons — rush forward, pressing against the windows. Before they are silenced, desperate screams course up through her vocal chords, fight their way into her throat, explode past her lips. Finally, Graxyl rears his head, letting out a roar of such ferocity that it shears the vehicle's metal body with stress cracks.

His last prowl nears its end with the clear distinction that he is still a 'monarch of the night.' And after a short, albeit terrifying, visit to Rob's house, job order Z81191F is complete — insuring that neither of the lovers lives 'happily ever after.'

JOB ORDER 21

MONSTER IN THE BRUSH

PALE LIGHT FROM A QUARTER MOON hanging low on the horizon renders mute the orange jumpsuit darting in-between the shadows and shallow cover of mesquite trees. When the sun reasserted itself the next morning there would be one less inmate at *Three Rivers* maximum-security federal penitentiary — specifically, inmate 821937.

Hector Rodriguez is in a race with the sunrise and the Mexico border, where he will find anonymity among a million other brown faces like his. When the initial rush of adrenalin subsided a few hours ago, crisp night air and fatigue transformed his legs into plodding cement logs. But Hector had anticipated this and purposefully detoured towards Choke Canyon Lake.

With yellow and orange leaves blanketing the asphalt, he does not expect to find many campers. But all he really needs is one. He slips into tall brush blanketing an embankment adjacent to the campground as the odor of a burning fire curls into his nostrils. His crooked, metal-clad teeth appear behind a crude smile as he crouches deeper under the cover of the long grass. Dropping onto all fours, he stealthily makes his way to the edge of the clearing.

Now on his belly, pushing aside blades of grass, his yellowed eyes pierce the darkness, fixing on the prize: a blue minivan just a few feet away from a roaring campfire. Hector's cracked lips spread into a grin. It seems almost too good to be true — a lone van and no other campers to potentially get in his way. There is, however, a 'problem.' It's not just a lone camper or two, but an entire family.

Hector folds his bottom lip beneath his top, mind churning for the next move. Silhouetted, their backs conveniently turned away from him, are the occupants of the vehicle: a man, a woman and a little girl. Both parents work around the fire cooking two little fish; their daughter cherubically sings campfire songs. Heartwarming to the core, it seems to be a moment taken directly from a Norman Rockwell painting. But only if Rockwell's paintings had also featured a five-time convicted murderer, waiting just beyond the edges of the frame. "Must not've been a very good day for fishing," Hector mutters under his breath. "And it looks like the night ain't gonna be much better."

Concealed in the dark gray contours brush-stroked across the clearing, Hector wriggles forward. His breathing is slow and shallow. It would be tough taking out the big ol' dad, so the trick will be to go for the little girl. After that everything should pretty much fall into place. So with the sound of singing becoming more distinct with every motion of his hand and foot, Hector reaches inside his boot, carefully removing a makeshift blade. Fixing it between his metal teeth, he slithers into the black, mottled clearing.

As his approach brings him closer to the campground, he's loath to acknowledge that firelight will soon yank away his cover of shadows. It was an adverse turn of circumstances, as shadows had been a reliable ally throughout the entirety of Hector's criminal existence. Now he would be completely exposed for a distance of at least 17 feet. With inches of darkness between his wiry frame and the orange light illuminating the rest of the campground, he hesitates. With his depraved mind busily contemplating alternative strategies, a 'miracle' falls into his lap: Father and Mother duck inside the tent for blankets and pillows.

Adrenalin rockets Hector to his feet and with time running slowly, he closes in on the little girl, swoops her up with one arm and levels the blade beneath her throat with the other. His twisted voice roars in unison with the campfire, "Come on out, Mami and Papi! I've got your niña!" His heart pounds hot and cold. "Now all I want...is the keys to your vehicle," he snarls. "Give 'em to me and everything'll be fine! (A lie) Screw with me and SLLIIITTT!" (The truth.)

Surprisingly, the little girl doesn't struggle or cry for help. In fact, Mother and Father seem slow emerging from the tent. Then, without warning, pain radiates through Hector's arm as tiny teeth sink deeply into muscle. Stumbling away from the campfire he howls in pain. His blade tumbles to the ground just as Mother erupts from the tent. With rhino-like ferocity she plants her head in Hector's chest, cartwheeling him into the air and back into the tall grass. Silence drapes itself over the camp.

Gazing down on Hector like a pack of nosy, speechless bystanders, the tall grass sways in the evening breeze. Wind knocked out of his lungs and staring into an unsympathetically black sky, Hector feels dread sink deep into his gut as two misshapen objects enter his field of vision: one little and the other large. Firelight flickers across the grotesque faces, fitted with huge jaws, flaring nostrils, long, spiked teeth and sunken eyes. Still on his back, Hector desperately attempts to scoot away, as excruciating pain shoots through his right leg. His femur is shattered. With blood still oozing from the bite mark on his arm, Hector whimpers like a bleating goat. "Get away from me you...you freaks!"

Recoiling slightly, the little girl fearfully inquires, "What is it, Mommy? It looks like a monster?" But before an answer can be given, grunts and growls are accompanied by the thud of feet plodding through the brush. In Hector's field of vision, the father goblin's massive, misshapen head, with a burning log hefted behind it, joins the two others.

SEVERAL HOURS LATER the quarter moon has climbed higher in the sky, along with the sounds of merriment and the swirling embers of the campfire. Smiling, the goblin father turns the spit slowly, careful to cook the meat evenly on all sides. Swaddled with blankets, the little goblin girl snuggles with Mother, sweetly humming to herself. It hadn't been the best of days for fishing, but it had certainly turned out to be an excellent night for barbecue.

CREATURE, II

B OOSTED ON HIS TWIN BROTHER'S SHOULDERS, Jóakim uses the sleeve of his thick flannel shirt to wipe condensation from the craft's top portal window. "Hurry up, man! You're heavy!" Július pleads. "Hold up a sec! I see something!" Jóakim is undeterred by his twin's typically cautious nature.

It's a handful of minutes past 9:00 and the moon is quickly replacing the sun in the slate and orange-tinged sky painted over Hrísey, Iceland. Július and Jóakim had hopped the ferry for the annual summer festival, and while out exploring, had found the odd-shaped vessel resting against the rocks of the rugged shoreline.

"J…I think there's a dude inside. Pulling myself up," shouts Jóakim.

"Come on bro, this thing looks like military," Then comes Jules well-worn protest: "Let's just report it," .

"And we will. But first let's have a look-see." Muscles tensed, Jóakim strains to break the door wheel free. "Jules, toss me up a piece of that rebar. See it? Over there." (Within seconds he's broken the wheel loose.) As the hatch swings open, the moon bathes a portion of the compartment with light, while leaving the rest charcoal-colored shapes and objects. Jóakim bangs the rebar on the lip of the opening, attempting to get a rise out of the slumped figure.

"Phew! It reeks! Whoever he is, I don't think he's with the living."

"Jóakim, let's go! Let's go!" His brother pleads.

"Waitaminnit! He moved! Jules! His arm! I'm goin' in!"

Before his brother can lodge another protest, Jóakim drops into the compartment. He kneels, allowing the moonlight to illuminate the man's body. "It's like he's got radiation poisoning or something." (Jóakim uses the crook of his arm to cover his nose). "Dude? You okay?" After a moment of hesitation, the man braces his arm against the floor, then painfully pushes his body upright.

"Where…am I?" Raw with pain, the man's voice barely rasps above a whisper.

"You're in Hrísey! Iceland! That's H-R-I-S-E-Y! The 'H' is silent!"

"What's he saying?" Shouts Július, apprehension building.

"F…f…f…" The man closes his eyes, struggling to form a few simple words.

"What is it mate? Whatcha trying to say?" Jóakim cautiously leans in towards the man's blackened lips.

"Full…" The man raises his mangled arm to shield his eyes. "…Moon?"

"Yeah, I'd say so," quips Jóakim. As he looks up and over his shoulder, he sees the full moon aligned perfectly with the airlock's opening. "He's beat up but still has a pretty full grasp of the obvious," Jóakim snickers back to his brother.

But as he returns his gaze to the vessel's interior his heart ticks up a notch. Bones in the man's face begin to bulge and protrude. His jaw line juts. Covering his face, the man screams. Wisely Jóakim steps back.

"Uhh Júles? Something's goin' down!" As he backs away more earnestly, Jóakim slips on the slime-coated floor, landing painfully on his rear. "Owwww!" He moans. Attempting to push himself back erect, he realizes that one of his hands has gotten wedged inside an object resting on the metal floor. Grasping a sturdy hold on it, he jerks his arm and the object forward — bringing him face-to-face with a decaying, oozing torso. With his hand stuck inside the rib cage, he thrashes the torso on the floor, accompanying each blow with an agitated shriek. Terror has seized him with what seems like an unyielding grip until a sound, a deep predatory growl, reclaims his attention.

Outside the craft, Július is terrified by the unearthly clamor emanating from the vessel. "J-Jóakim, what's happening?" Július stammers, struggling to climb a craft with no adequate footholds. Then with a dreadful howl and absolutely no warning, the decaying werewolf emerges from the airlock, sniffs the air, bares its teeth and pounces. The attack is fierce and red.

As the melee continues a smaller werewolf emerges from the airlock, jumps to the ground, then rests on its haunches. No more than a few moments expire before a third creature joins the pack. The alpha cocks its nose to the air: A familiar scent carries on the swirling summer winds — intoxicating, pungent, raw. No vocal communication is needed. On all fours, the werewolf zombies gallop rapaciously towards the village.

NAVIGATING THE STRAIT of Eyjafjörður and just a short distance from the landing, Viggo Nyström, the ferry's night captain, notices a violent commotion amongst the waiting passengers. He raises binoculars and his unbelieving eyes sight three ferocious creatures hungrily assaulting one victim after another. Less than seven passengers are present below deck, but as the ship's captain they are his responsibility. Nyström is torn between protecting those onboard and saving what is left of the passengers on the landing.

However, the opportunity to formulate an equitable strategy disappears when, abruptly, sniffing the air, one of the creatures senses new prey. Through the binoculars, Nyström's eyes meet those of the werewolf. He spins the boat's wheel and reverses its engine — too late! Binoculars tremble as Nyström watches the werewolf, bounding on all fours, race down the dock and hurtle onboard.

Crashing through the ship's bridge window, the werewolf tackles Nyström. Unmanned, the ferry continues throttling backwards into the strait. But the creature quickly discovers this victim is not going down without a fight. With what appears to be adrenalin-charged strength, Nyström shoves the werewolf into a tangle of life preservers. Passengers startled by the commotion venture upstairs and then scatter just as quickly. Nyström clasps his palms and begins swinging his arms, smashing the werewolf's face fiercely. On the edge of the staircase leading down into the empty passenger hold the punch-drunk werewolf tumbles.

At the bottom, groggily, the werewolf's eyes focus. Before it can react, a backlit outline of Nyström, arms spread, sailing through the air, lands crouching on top of him. With a dash of sophistication and a hint of theatrics, the vampire tilts its head back and contemptuously sinks its fangs deep into the werewolf's neck. Outside the ferry a heavy dark rain pounds the coastline.

CREATURE, II 29

L IKE MOST 14-YEAR-OLDS, Max Stein exists at the very edge of the age where a young boy still worships his father. Unfortunately, Franklin was always a stubbornly difficult man to idolize. Standing a frail but commanding 6-foot-6, he required hours of solitude to fully concentrate on his experiments. In fact, Max was something of an 'accident.'

Bluntly and when Max was only 6 years of age, Franklin revealed that he was the unfortunate result of a 12-month polar expedition, an attractive female colleague and a hazy evening of vodka shots. "You were an experiment that went very, very bad," Max was told. So with soaring stacks of regrets cluttering the elder Stein's life, there was scarce room for a 14-year-old.

It was at night, with strange sounds and yellow light emanating from the windows of his father's backyard workshop, that Max could finally be 'with' his father. Drifting in through his third-story window, the mysterious sounds would draw Max's bare feet out of bed and onto the cold hardwood floor, to the cool prickly backyard grass and finally up to the dusty workshop window. For hours he'd watch his father work, daring Franklin not to see him. To Max, his father was a genius.

But to his father, Max was an annoying stray puppy, better off euthanized than having to continue its wretched existence. Then on one particular Friday, as Franklin slouched in a faded overstuffed chair, the 'yapping' began again.

"Father, your microwave dinner's been prepared." Max's voice is barely above a whisper, aching for approval.

"Place it there." His father motions, pointing at a TV table but continuing to scribble notes. "And my drink? Where is it, Half-Wit?"

"I'm sorry, I'm sorry. Getting it now." Max slinks back to the kitchen, quickly emerging with a tall glass of liquid. "Father, I kinda wanted to let you know, in biology, I'm at the top of my class…" Walking carefully across the thick green carpet, Max thinks his father is like an unpredictable old dog. Yet somehow, he finds the confidences to continue: "…and I absolutely destroyed my chemistry midterm."

"Really?" Is his father's quizzical response. Then, a rare occurrence happens: Franklin interrupts his studies and looks at the boy through the top of his reading glasses. "Is that so?"

As an understated smile barely conceals the boy's braces, Franklin realizes that in many ways, Max is a gangly version of his younger self (with the exception of the spiky hair and ridiculous gauges sitting in both earlobes). A rare tinge of pride softens the near permanent crease in Franklin's brow. Maybe the 'Half-Wit' is more brilliant than he'd given him credit for. Maybe it was time for the boy to start assisting with experiments.

If only Max could've heard these budding thoughts of admiration. Regrettably, just before he reaches the chair, Father's glowing musings are drenched as Max's toe catches a snag, sending the glass tumbling onto his father's precious diagrams. The harsh berating that follows leaves deep scars, invisible, but no less painful than the ones he'd earn from the beating — and then banishment.

Chained in the cavernous basement, illuminated by a single pull-string lamp, Max does what he's always done: sob into his folded arms. But this night his tears fuel a deep, gnawing rage that he now realizes has been smoldering within him for quite some time. Finding a blunt tool, he pries open the shackle fixed to his ankle and next the heavy padlock to the walk-in freezer. In wintertime, between long stretches of solitude, he'd begun his own 'project.' Now it is time to finish it. He exits the freezer with four unwieldy butcher paper-wrapped bundles. Then with the movement of a large electrical throw switch, the old basement lab hums to life.

Sunday night arrives, a key works the basement door and a putrid odor immediately greets Franklin's nose. "Did you get into my freezer, Half-Wit?" Eyes darting wildly, the very mad scientist thunders down the creaky wooden stairs. "Where are you, boy?" Twenty-five watts of illumination barely stretches across the room, revealing a spiky mop of dishwater-blonde hair. "How'd you get that shackle loose, boy? Huh? Huh! Get your sorry butt over here!"

On the opposite side of the room Max furtively crouches in the shadows. "You really want this don't you? You're going to make me have to hurt you!" Striding forward, Franklin tightens his fist as if he is preparing for a street fight. The saturated tones of rage distort his vision. A little more than halfway across the room, Max's brown eyes lock with his: "No, Father. This is going to hurt you."

Rising from the shadows, the boy's frame towers inexplicably over his father's head. The elder Stein stumbles backwards, kicking and swinging his fists in the air. Through loose bandages Franklin's awe-struck eyes glimpse heavy black stitches connecting grotesquely long legs and brawny thick arms to the boy's skinny torso. Overcome with astonished horror, he desperately crawls for the wooden staircase. Franklin manages to scramble only a short distance before Max's muscular arm extends from the shadows and firmly grips the scruff of his neck. With eyes growing ever wider, Franklin is ferried back across the room, to directly face his mutilated son. With deep sincerity and a voice barely above a whisper, Max apologizes: "I'm sorry about this, Father." Then with one thudding slap, Franklin is unconscious.

MONTHS LATER the atmosphere at the Stein home is much improved. As always, Max has brought dinner to the overstuffed chair. "Enjoy your dinner, Father?" (He inquires happily.) "Yes. Thank you, Son." (Returns a tired voice.) "So Father, can we work in the shop tonight?" (He smiles.) "Of course, Son. Anything you'd like." (It is the right and only answer.) Max reaches down to unlock the shackle on Franklin's ankle. "I've learned so much from you," he says, hefting his father onto his shoulder like a giant rag doll. "I guess it's as they say, 'Like father, like son.'"

the
FLASH

THE LIFE RAFT

AMBER STROBE LIGHTS PULSE, alternately illuminating the two tired faces tenuously straddling the wreckage. Forty-eight hours had passed, maybe 72. It's hard to tell with growing delirium and gnawing hunger fogging the two men's minds.

The life vest strobes are the only lights visible from the epicenter of the crash all the way out to the featureless horizon. It all happened so quickly: A loud thump. Frightened voices over the intercom. Oxygen masks. Panic. Depressurization. Rapid descent. Life vests. Screams. Impact.

"Tosh?" coughs Alejandro, huddled on the makeshift deck. "You think we're gonna make it? You think anyone's comin' for us?"

"I am very sure that the pilot would have radioed our position before we went down. They will find us. We will be fine." As required by his culture, Sitoshi's words are even and confident. In reality, it is bravado.

Sitoshi Matsuko is a businessman who was en route from a consumer electronics show in Amsterdam. When he heard the thump, he was sitting in business class and had just taken a generous slurp of a single malt. Alejandro Saez, on the other hand, was nobody. Just another of the row-upon-row of non-descript faces sardined into coach class. He'd taken a sip of flat tonic water when he heard the thump. Fortuitously, the lives of these two men are now inextricably connected by the events that have produced the mangled wreckage upon which they now sit.

The previous morning they managed to recover a refreshment cart full of beverages. There was no food, but it was better than nothing. The following morning Alejandro spied an emergency kit attached to one of the planes exit hatches. Alejandro risked a dive into the tempestuous sea to retrieve it. Unfortunately salt water had seeped inside, rendering most of its contents unusable. But the flare gun worked.

Now at nightfall, a gale has blown in, mercilessly pelting the disheartened men with freezing rain. Buffeted by the steep onyx waves, their 'raft' is swiftly and steadily taking on water. Sitoshi earned a nasty gash on his left calf when Alejandro first pulled him from the water. And as the improvised bandage has loosened, the wound is leaving behind a waterborne trail of blood. Cloud cover and a drizzling sky obscure the moon's light, rendering the crimson trail invisible to the two men. But it does not go unnoticed by—

"Sharks!" Exclaims Alejandro, quickly edging to the top of the raft.

"Oh no! Two more! Behind you!" Panics Sitoshi.

"Move! Get into the middle of the raft…" And then Alejandro's voice trails off.

Less than yards away, emerging from the blackness, a monstrous dorsal fin protrudes 5 feet above the surface of the ocean and then disappears. Fear rapidly drains the air from Alejandro's lungs as he whispers under his breath: "We're screwed." At the edge of the raft, Sitoshi's wounded leg and a slick deck make movement difficult. He barely drags himself forward as the shark's massive head erupts from the black waters, its jaws pulverizing a 4-foot section of the raft. Equilibrium lost, Sitoshi tumbles into the churning waves.

"No!" Alejandro's scream is raw. Cutting its tailfin left, the monstrous creature swings its massive body around for another pass. Wisely, the smaller sharks keep their distance. Slipping and skidding back to the front of the raft, Alejandro fumbles in the emergency survival kit: The flare gun.

"Oh, God, help me!" Pleads a wide-eyed Sitoshi. As he glances back, in tiny snapshots, his flashing strobe reveals the killing machine opening its jaws, exposing layers of blade-like teeth. With death just over Sitoshi's shoulder, Alejandro fires directly into the shark's gaping maw. "Die, monster! Die!" Rolling onto its side, the creature disappears below the surface. "Gimme your hand!" Hollers Alejandro.

But with predatory intelligence the shark emerges at the back of the raft, brushing its bottom and knocking Alejandro off-balance. The flare gun tumbles, sliding to the other end of the raft. With seawater rushing into its open jaws, the shark puts itself on course for the flailing Sitoshi. Desperately, Alejandro rockets on his stomach across the slippery deck, aiming his outstretched arm for the fallen gun. Hand closing around the slippery muzzle, he loads the last flare, aiming it toward Sitoshi's cries.

The flare's short trajectory plunges it deep into the creature's gills. If the shark had vocal chords, it surely would have bellowed a fearsome cry. Instead it thrashes, rolls onto its back and almost noiselessly slips beneath the agitated waters. Black becomes red. Within seconds the feeding frenzy begins. Within minutes it ends. And for the first time in three days, the rain lets up.

EXHAUSTED AND LYING ON ACHING BACKS, the men are heartened as a large hopeful moon reveals itself from behind quickly dissipating clouds. "I think the worse is over," Sitoshi wearily wheezes. "I mean, after all of this, someone must certainly be watching over our souls."

Sitting up, Alejandro says nothing, quickly burying his head in folded arms. "You okay, my friend?" Sitoshi asks with concerned apprehension. "I…I can't. I'm sorry…" Alejandro chokes out in between tears. Sliding forward, Sitoshi places both hands on Alejandro's shoulders. "What is it? Let me help you!" Alejandro's entire body is beginning to shake violently. "He's seizing!" Sitoshi thinks out loud, desperately searching for the emergency kit. But as Alejandro raises his head aloft it is clear that he is not the one in need of help. For the second time that night Sitoshi says the words: "Oh, God, help me!" Then (flash) face contortions (flash) hair growth (flash) rabid growling (flash) fangs.

The werewolf's attack is feral and lightning fast.

Moments later, as the creature sits alone on the makeshift raft, a small wave of regret washes through its virulent mind. The two men had survived so much together. So much. But the reality is quite clear: He is a werewolf and after three days at sea, he was hungry enough to eat a cow — or at the very least, Sitoshi.

GLASS JARS

I 'LL ASK YOU ONE MORE TIME to get your feet moving up out of my store," snaps the crusty old proprietor. He jabs his bony finger at the hand-written sign below the register: No exchanges. No refunds. "You know, McKinnon, this town has supported you for over 40 years," the man says, shaking his head. "And what have you given us? You don't open until noon, seems like your prices go up every other week and the only thing worse than the prices is your attitude."

"Now I'm not gonna say this three times, Caleb: Get up out of my store before I make you pay your account in full — right this instant. You want that?" With his dignity laid bare, Caleb retreats, exiting the store.

"Didn't think so," McKinnon mutters.

With red suspenders stretched over his bony frame, he shuffles towards the back storeroom. Regrettably, *McKinnon's Hardware and General Store* is the only true retail establishment in the township of Burwell, Nebraska. This affords Egeus McKinnon wide latitude in the way he runs his business. He chuckles to himself: No one had summoned the gumption to talk to him like that in a very long time. There would be a price to pay. His shuffle quickens as he walks past the rows of aged storage shelves leading to the back of the structure.

Reaching into his shirt pocket, he pulls out a patina-encrusted key, fiddling briefly with the padlock clamped to the metal ring securing the wooden door. When he reaches the bottom of the cellar, his steely gray eyes survey a room of shelves stacked three deep with large, cobweb-encrusted jars.

McKinnon is what is known as a "Keeper."

Placing his wrinkled palm against a jar, he smears away a thick accumulation of dust. As he peers inside the inch-thick glass, pride thaws his cold eyes. McKinnon has the glow of a parent who's proudly watched his offspring grow from child to adult. In a warped sense his pride is understandable. This jar represents one of the best of his breeding efforts — perfection really. Repeating the same one-handed dusting, he studiously examines the contents of an assortment of the jars. Some receive an "X" scrawled in dust. The "X"s travel down the ladder with McKinnon.

As he carefully loads his pickup, it's rather telling that the jars selected are from the topmost shelves: Maximum potency.

Later, a little past midnight, McKinnon rises, reviews a crinkled map and heads out. Covered in wrinkles, sunspots and strands of white hair, his arm rests on the truck's open window frame. As the warm evening air flows through what is left of his formerly thick mane, McKinnon is reminded of how much he enjoys this time of evening. Aside from the melodious chirping of cicadas, the entire town is tucked in under blankets. As the dusty Ford makes its way past row after row of picket fences, nostalgia overtakes McKinnon: At one time or another, he's visited every last one of these homes.

Rounding a corner and braking to a stop, he places the column shifter in 'park.' Quietly swinging the door open, he carefully places one boot, then another into the tread -grooved alley. The black tarp used to conceal the jars he folds and sets aside.

As his wizened legs carry him forward, he feels the creatures' wings beat restlessly against the glass jars cradled in his arms. Bony fingers pry open the wooden windowsill and then quietly unscrew the metal jar tops. As the Vaporghoul senses its imminent release, its eyes glow iridescently purple. McKinnon has seen this transformation thousands of times, but it still fascinates him to watch the creatures deconstruct their bodies into molecules light enough to be carried underneath the cracked sill — and straight into the nostrils of the slumbering victim.

A single Vaporghoul infesting a person's mind creates nightmares. Two: Night terrors. Three: Temporary insanity. Having set the three empty jars on the ground, McKinnon peers into the room. Like purplish-green gnats, the Vaporghoul's molecules swirl in a vortex with the small end of the funnel entering one nostril of Caleb's nose. He stirs. Then inhales, readying a sneeze. Of course, Vaporghouls secrete an enzyme that temporarily stifles this reflex. In seconds his languid limbs retract, then, seizing, shoot out in all directions. McKinnon's knurled fingers tremble in a hasty effort to slide the window shut before raw screams escape, souring an otherwise pleasant summer evening.

AT 4AM HE RETURNS for his pets. With one jar under his arm, he climbs the rungs of the ladder, carefully returning the last of the Vaporghouls to the shelf. He muses on how comical it had been to see such a tall and forceful man curled in the fetal position alongside his bed, drooling and babbling nonsense. It had been a very good night, he decides.

However, as McKinnon slowly backs down the ladder, a dust accumulation on one of the rungs sends his foot slipping. McKinnon grabs at the shelves to steady his balance, but, too late, the ladder has swung out from under him! His bony hands grip the top shelf tenuously. Distressed he eyes the masonry screws holding the shelves to the wall, wondering how long they will hold. But before the screws can give way the wooden shelves moan, buckling under weight they were never intended to support.

Then everything goes black.

Crumpled on his side, McKinnon regains consciousness. His eyes slowly focus on thousands of glass shards scattered around his body. Painfully, he rolls onto his back. The air is thick and electric. He feels a tickle in one nostril and then the other. A tear beads and streams down his left cheek. McKinnon's eyes roll back under his eyelids, his body violently jerks, convulses, and scant moments later, his eyes go to static — like a television without a signal.

McKinnon's Hardware and General Store never re-opened. And curiously, not a soul in dusty little Burwell, Nebraska, ever spoke of having a nightmare again.

CREATURE, III

VERNIGHT, UNUSUALLY HEAVY SLEET has swept in from the Atlantic and currently pounds the South End of Halifax. Today, however, nasty weather is not what has riveted the attention of Nova Scotians.

"...The UK-based snack company is recalling over 2,500 packages of gourmet beef jerky," warns the concerned BBC news anchor, "believed to have been made from livestock infected with mad cow disease. Now, while most of the tainted snacks have been accounted for, it is feared a small amount may have ended up in gift packages destined for Royal Navy servicemen. Iain Jones has the story."

Owen R. MacRae stabs the remote control, switching the large flat screen to black. Removing his tie, he wonders to himself how "that fool company" could have been so careless. Martini in hand, he strides across the room to a floor-to-ceiling glass window overlooking the bay. Placing the cocktail aside, he uses the sleeve of his tailored dress shirt to remove condensation from a portion of the window.

Peering through the tempestuous gale, MacRae blinks, then shakes his head. To his disbelief and not too far in the distance, the shape of a hideous, decaying creature emerges from the sleet-driven storm — each beat of its powerful wings bringing it into clearer focus. With a slight tremor, MacRae's hand finds the martini, raising it to his lips for one final sip. Moments later, a creature from the blackest recesses of nightmares smashes through the window.

Accompanied by a deafening boom and splintered glass shards, the Creature exits MacRae's residence with chaos and death eagerly following it to the street below. At times it swoops from the air to assault its victims or alternately runs on all fours to attack. Regardless of the method, the final kill is accomplished with fangs to the throat.

As nightfall and gruesome death cast their long shadows across the peninsula, Canadian Forces Primary Reserve have no choice but to pull back. Skulking unchallenged through the vacant neighborhoods, wings tucked, the Creature shatters windows and ransacks homes in search of new victims. Its nose sniffs the air, only detecting trace scents of human flesh. But as the wind shifts direction an acrid odor wafts into its nostrils — a scent just on the tip of its forked tongue.

A Prowler.

Like a crazed linebacker, the Prowler blasts out of nowhere, slamming the Creature into a cement retaining wall. Hastily unfolding its wings, the Creature takes to flight, dragging the Prowler aloft. Cognizant of its vulnerability as the Creature continues gaining more dizzying altitude, the Prowler reaches around, brutally tearing loose the left wing. Spinning like a ghastly maple seed, the two monsters plummet to the ground, exchanging blows all the way.

Demolishing a nearby fountain on impact, the Creature savagely darts for the Prowler's pulsing jugular vein — only to have its efforts fended off by a slash of the Prowler's lethal claws. Quickly recovering, the Creature's fangs find an arm. Wincing in pain, the Prowler emits a howl so intense it shatters every pane of glass within a two-block radius. In one motion the Prowler lifts the Creature, hurling it into a jumble of power lines. Entangled and struggling to free itself of the electrified spiderweb, wisps of smoke rise from the Creature's brownish-gray pelt. Its cry is a shriek: Penetrating and shrill. At the same time a roar of victory is in order for the Prowler.

Flexing like a steroid-fueled body builder, the Prowler's victory is quickly cut short by the realization that infection is rapidly spreading from the puncture wound on its arm. Untwisting itself from the power lines, the Creature tumbles to the pavement in a tangled heap of wings and fangs. The dawn of its foe's defeat has suddenly appeared on the horizon. Gripping its wounded arm, the Prowler stumbles to one knee.

A short distance away, the Creature preserves its advantage by skittering into a partially demolished structure. By now the fast-moving infection has nearly engulfed the Prowler's body. And with a grand, reverberating thud, it collapses onto the wet pavement. Beads of hail immediately begin to accumulate around its body.

Cloaked in shadows, the glowing eyes of the Creature narrow with delight. With the battlefield quieted, its nose cautiously emerges, sniffing the air for the odor of death. It inhales deeply, pulling every scent in the vicinity across its olfactory nerve. None match. Then, abruptly, with a heave of its massive chest, the Prowler slowly lifts its head. As it painfully rises to its feet, with each leaden step forward, its immune system purges the infection from its bloodstream.

In rabid desperation, luck no longer on its side, the Creature bounds from the shadows. Even in the world of monsters it is an abomination, ill-suited for any real purpose. It must no longer exist.

Galloping at full speed, the two creatures engage. Wrapping its wing and two arms around the Prowler's torso, the Creature bears down with all its might, its claws sinking deeply into the Prowler's hide. Curiously, the Prowler does not struggle. It does not return blows. It doesn't even roar. Instead, with one savage twist, the Prowler rips the Creature's head from its body. Claws retracting, the wing and arms of the Creature fall limp. However, a curtain has not yet been drawn on this grisly production.

Almost as quickly as it was removed, the head begins regenerating. Fully determined to bring the battle to a close, the Prowler roars from deep within its chest and then with great force plunges its main horn straight through the Creature's heart.

A LITTLE MORE THAN WINDED, Graxyl sprawls himself across the pavement, chest heaving with exhaustion. Up until now, retirement in Halifax was great, the climate perfect: Frigid and rainy. In all of his 464 years he'd never encountered anything quite like the Creature. Fortunately for him, just the day before, he'd visited the dentist. And, as it turns out his decaying horn had been in urgent need of new silver fillings.

NIC KRISTOFER BLACK is a writer, graphic designer, filmmaker and insomniac residing in Los Angeles, California. His writing is influenced by the classic horror films of Universal Pictures as well as an unhealthy dose of EC Comics, Twilight Zone and X-Files episodes. He dabbles in all things creative and would like to try neon art the next time he has a spare moment.

JORGE GONZALEZ is an illustrator and graphic designer residing in Venezuela. When he's not busy creating alien landscapes, creatures and concept art, he loves good movies, videogames and anything Star Wars related. Check out some of the other cool stuff he's done at www.artstation.com/artist/antonjorch.

internegative